Serenade

Serenade

Janet M. Izzo

Bric-a-Brac

Press

Bric-a-Brac

Press

Bric-a-Brac Press

Copyright © 2024 Janet M. Izzo

Cover art and design: Rebecca Bowman

Book design: Rebecca Bowman

ISBN: 9781961136045

Shady Grove is a traditional folk song in the public domain.

The verses on pages 77 and 81 were translated into English from the song lyrics by poet Julio Numhausen for "Todo cambia."

The epigraph on page 47 comes from Annie Dillard's novel *Pilgrim at Tinker Creek.*

For Sigfrido

The Banjo

The Lake

The baby sleeps in a banjo case left open. The lullaby, a constant drone amidst rhythmic banter.

If we are all mestizos, the banjo follows the pattern of tales of immigration and transformation, trauma and indignities.

At the risk of being defined by the voyage, we seek the seed. The country of origin. History rewinds itself until the last frame rests on the opposite shore. A continent before trading slaves. An Africa consumed in its daily present. Practical and persistent in its traditions.

A *banjar* from West Africa. Simple shapes intersect. A line. A sphere. A gourd penetrated by a strung pole. Animal skin humming. A clever collaboration of percussion and strings. A hybrid. A prediction.

A meandering rhythm setting you awandering. Releasing you before you arrive. Back at the point of departure, that much the wiser.

1

They never intended to steal a culture along with its people. Perhaps the first trespasser never listened to their music. Unable to see beyond the color of skin and money. Unable to hear a voice identified as purely human. Leaving the angels to weep.

∞

The baby wakes. Recognizing the bump-ditty cadence as her father's presence. The banjo case her bed. Picks and broken strings scattered beside her. She is well accompanied, secure in her closed set of familiar objects.

Secure in the familiar woods of the East Coast. An area defined by the Hudson Valley. Water and a ritual of seasons.

Her father arrives late from his job in the city. Quiet and distracted. Before his late evening meal, he grabs his banjo. She makes a request. *Shady Grove* lulls her to sleep as his eyes close. He repeats the rhythm, chasing the day from his thoughts.

If she lies still at night, she can feel the rumble of the passing train, frailing against the steel tracks, a recognizable beat accompanying her fragile breath into sleep.

∞

Went to see my Shady Grove
Standing in the door.
Shoes and stockings in her hand
Little bare feet on the floor.

∞

A banjo is placed in her lap. She strums the simple trio of an ancestral rhythm: Bump-ditty, bump-ditty, bump-ditty.

Her thumb lowers to the shortest string. Her middle finger lowers further, to the string farthest from her. Brushing it with the back of her fingernail. Then continuing, hammering the animal skin. Held tight by metal clamps. Coarse through thin pajamas.

She hums to the strings as she plays, keeping time. But time passes.

∞

For Christmas, her father builds her a wooden framed banjo, smooth against her thighs. Black ebony fingerboard. Fretless. A horizon of possibilities. Made to measure against her small frame.

Starting from stillness, she reaches for the tuning pegs. Matches the intervals she hears. No spoken instructions. *The old gray goose is dead.* Never learning the names of the notes. *She died in the mill pond.* Fingers follow fingers. *Standing on her head.*

Bump-ditty. Three beats. Four hands.

∞

Splash. Step. Splash. Cool against her legs, tempering the morning heat. Her morning task is to fetch the drinking water from the cast iron pump. Down the hill.

Taking small steps under the weight of the bucket, she watches the ground in front of her. Wary of snakes darting from the bushes beside the path. She changes hands. The bucket handle digging into her soft palm.

She passes the clearing where her father gutted and cleaned the morning's catch. Where they examined the fish's stomach to decipher its last meal. The fish they will grill for breakfast.

∽

Every early morning, they fish. The mist on the lake hides the muted paddle, dipping into unseen water. A deliberate stroke repeated. In silence.

Her hand drags alongside the canoe. Smooth canvas against her arm.

They search the illusive catch of the summer. The dream of a bass so big she fears its capture.

The fishing line guides the hushed fall of the fly. Dropped deftly as a craftsman adding the final details. Dropped near the last sighting of the prey. Blue heron as witness.

She rearranges the flies in their blue box. Ten compartments. Five by two. Sheltered beneath a clear plastic lid.

There is a light blue fly with midnight head and
    zebra mane,
a copper fly with a translucent sliver of wings and
    iridescent blue body,
a black metallic fly with magenta tail,
an auburn fly with black head and scarlet tail,
an elegant bright yellow fly with modest yellow
    wings,
a silvery brown fly with golden body and short
    deep red tail,
another just the same but with a thicker spiraled
    body and longer red tail,
a fly, all cream colored but with a dark body,
a white fly with three wings
and one compartment left empty.
The one that got away.

The flies lie safe and separate. Still in their show-
case. Her vision of precious. They inhabit her
dreams. Buzzing like mosquitos but without men-
ace. Seeking nothing if not freedom. Leading the
way through the open window into the darkness of
an undreamed future.

∞

After fishing, they follow the shore of a small island as she collects blueberries. So sweet and so cold. In an old tin can. Careful not to drop them into the lake.

They avoid the rocks as the canvas of the canoe is delicate, pulled tight over ribs of wood. The water grows shallow near the shore. But the mist has lifted, and the bottom is clear.

∞

The banjo and canoe share a common seed and evolution. They have been pursued and continue to pursue us. Entwined in our history. Periodically resurfacing. As if searching for air.

Whether it be dug out of a tree trunk or shaped from a wooden frame covered in birch bark, the canoe has always been a vessel. A mode of transportation. At times, migration.

Still today, it represents the quiet choice amidst predominant motors. Its slight wake almost unperceivable. Developed to simply cut through the waters and, skillful as a surgeon, mend its wound almost immediately.

Before Columbus, canoes could be found in the Americas. As well as in Africa. Shared methods of pure expediency. Fundamental. Carefully balanced. Though threatened. Appropriated for a new set of imposing needs. Mistakenly called their own.

∞

She builds the canoe with her father in their carport. The neighborhood children gather to watch them. Sneaking back at night to slip in and out of the skeletal structure.

To say she builds the canoe is perhaps only her perception. She is very young, not yet attending school. She hands him tools and knows to keep near.

It is his first canoe yet he seems an expert. Following written instructions seamlessly. Rarely needing to correct a mistake.

He asks her to lie across the curved frame. To look into the sky as he narrates what to expect afloat: The wisp of a cloud. A swallow. The dance of a fishing line. Lightning.

From the belly of the beast, she naps. The unfinished vessel her dream. No need for more than this bare structure. No need for more than promises of exploration and sanctuary.

The wood varnished. The canvas stretched and painted. A flying Canadian goose stenciled behind her father's cushioned seat.

∞

He built the banjo and the canoe. One wood and skin. Tight as a drum. The other wood and canvas. Watertight.

He built the banjo and the canoe. One an instrument to be held. The other a hollowed vessel. Both subtle in their resonant alcoves.

Decades later, upon her father's death, she deliberates. If only she could send him off as he deserved. If only we could create our own rites though our voice be silenced. She would lay him delicately in that vessel, his back against the bowed ribs. Face toward the sky. His banjo in his arms. Shown the way by a solitary goose. Headed for home.

∽

Shady Grove, my little love
Shady Grove I say.
Shady Grove, my little love
I'm bound to go away.

∽

Back to the hill, the water pump behind her. She shakes earlier morning adventures and distant premonitions from her head. Carefully continues toward the house. Bucket splashing.

Water slippers threatening to abandon her feet. Heals scraping the ground.

She enters the kitchen. Lifts the bucket to the counter. Grabs the ladle and drinks the cool water. Allowing it to drip down her chin to the floor.

∽

Next, she waters the flowers. She fills her watering can with lake water and tends to the plants surrounding the hammock. Careful to keep her distance from the dark green cloth with white fringe. Fitted tightly over a rusted metal structure.

She once spent early evenings swaying in that hammock. Playing her banjo. Watching the sky turn pink as the scent of sliced cantaloupe and instant coffee reached her small garden from the picnic table. Adults half filling long benches.

That was before the encounter. The rock in her path. When things lost their fluidity.

An irreversible break with no definition but sorrow over something lost.

∞

I kneel
At the lake's edge
Playing softly
To calm the waters.
Eyes closed
To the sound of falling
Over stones and sticks
Over frets and bridges
Over decades

And centuries
Beyond my memory.
Bump-ditty.
Bump.

∞

It is impossible to forget debts to be paid.

Across the ocean, an ocean of time away. Dust rises between huts and heat. Right hand tight as a claw, hammering both strings and skin.

Back when the banjo was simply defined. Not a migrant. Unviolated. A single strain. Not bound for *Shady Grove* yet a well rooted clearing, nonetheless. Home.

A lullaby of a distinctive vernacular echoes.
Unaware and unable to envision the travesties of minstrel shows and painted faces gathering crowds beyond their village.

A perverse misappropriation. Wearing the banjo as if a necklace of pocketed pearls.

The Bass

The City

Thunder warns. Lightning strikes. A spark gives life to a modern-day monster in the making. The guitar becomes electric. An experiment that borders insanity. Unstoppable in its repercussions.

The guitar evolves. Its neck stretches. Sheds two strings. Its voice lowering an octave.

Solid as a foundation. Steady as a heartbeat. Beet red, her bass.

∞

Sitting on a black vinyl sofa. Spinning the record a notch slower. Listening hard for an almost unperceivable bassline. She remembers then repeats.

Her eyes close in relaxed concentration. Patiently melting into the source of her inspiration: BB and his guitar, Lucille. The king and queen. The thrill of it.

Their improvisations bring her home. The solo guitar constant in its wandering. Her bass allowing, extending an implied promise. Granting permission for digression.

She learns the bass to play the blues. The blues reach something within her. Then twist deeper.

She practices. Skipping parallel strings. Alternating adjacent fingerings. The same fret, a dissonant exercise.

She unearths the visual patterns of the scales. Their repetition, her fixation. Ascending, then finding solace in the lower strings. Sensing the vibrations, the more inaudible they descend.

Her bass is red, named Blue. An Epiphone, scaled to size. Five foot two. Blue jeans. Red suede Pumas. Her long hair cut short.

They will see how resilient she is and be ashamed. She plays wanting, waiting to be part of a whole. Feeling unbroken playing vinyl on vinyl. Sticking to the hot summer nights.

∞

A guitarist chooses the blues.
The bassist is blue.
There's no escaping it.
Dues or no dues paid.

∞

Before the Second World War, the electric bass started percolating. A body rendered solid, then fretted and lowered to a horizontal position. But it wasn't until well after the war when the electric bass became more popular. Started gaining traction. To be seen as something less than an abomination.

Standup basses were impractical. They were weighty and presented considerable complications. A subway turnstile. The steep steps of a bus. Rush hour crowds.

What's more, approaches and venues had evolved. The traditional double bass lingered. Inaudible amidst an increasingly amplified environment. Unable to surface from the depths.

A high price to pay, you may say, leaving the beloved double bass behind. Its animated profile, unambiguously human.

The electric bass kept tight company nonetheless. And embrace it she does. Even in its new configuration, it proves hard to handle for a young girl with hands struggling to travel the frets. Barely reaching to tune that last string.

∾

In her mind, she visualizes the neighborhood. Block by block. Remembering every building. The number of floors. The color of graffiti. Aware of dangers and past experiences she wishes to avoid. Crowds gathering at unlit corners. Piles of dirty snow camouflaging ice.

She is aware of internal red lights. Bombarding then guiding her intuition. Aware of the danger but equally aware of an irrefutable undertaking. She counts her steps and continues.

Before she steps off the bus, she reruns the route in her mind. Cross the street in the middle of the block. Then back again at the abandoned building.

Trying hard to remember which streetlights were burnt or broken. Connecting the dots. Sometimes missing a few. Then reconnecting.

We learn from a young age how to maneuver the dangers. Scanning the street ahead while keeping present of the ground beneath our feet. We make eye contact without salutation. Our eyes neutral. Moving on. Beyond. No matter how frightened. Unsettled we actually feel.

We perform through confrontation. No wandering perceivable in our stride. We know where we are going and absorb the trauma. Another layer. Hard as armor.

∽

I have heard the warrior cry
Only to be soothed by primitive lullabies.
They are guilty
And whisper no white lies.
I know what I hear.

∽

In the middle of the next block, after the empty lot, a naked bulb lights the entrance to the club. The front window of the building is decorated with faded gold leafing. Testimony to the neighborhood's layered past. It is brick. Five floors. 267 steps from the bus stop. The bouncer watches her.

Just a kid. Obviously underage. She enters the club. Eyes focused, through smoke, on the musicians. The music draws her to the front table. Cushions her seat.

Granting an illicit permission, the waitress places a drink on the table. The extra chair is removed. The beat carries her. Her apprehension sheds. Shoulders fall.

She concentrates on the tune. *Giant Steps* taken faster than she is accustomed to. She struggles to keep up. Trusts her teacher. He plays guitar. Leads the band.

At the break, they quiz her. Inquiring what she's heard. What she didn't hear. Themes and variations. Transitions and modulations. The bassist asks what she's been working on. She walks straight into his trap. An invitation. Reluctance.

Then ultimate agreement.

She slips onto the stage. Lowers the stool. His bass, a Fender Precision. The neck is longer, thicker. Presenting an expected challenge.

∞

Her teacher nods.
Simple blues.

No smoke.
No mirrors.

She becomes unstrung.
The bass becomes her.

∞

Outside. Snow falls. She has no idea how she will get home. The snow renders a misleading innocence to whatever it touches. Nothing actually changes. Merely lies dormant.

She forces herself to pay attention. Begins to walk home. Hood over her head. Scarf tied loosely around her neck. She reigns in her excitement from the performance. Stares straight ahead.

She has no money for the subway, not to mention a taxi. It will take her all night to walk home. She is not made of sugar. Walks the walk as her two fingers would walk a bass line. Calloused. Used to playing hard.

∞

But what I want to know is why
Hand me a cotton dress
And virgin's gloves
When mine
Is a polar expedition?

∞

Snow continues to fall. The structure of *Giant Steps* runs through her mind. Chord changes stand witness to generations of inspiration and hardships.

Whether or not the streets are paved, theirs is a primal struggle. She accepts the challenge as if honored. Accepts it, knowing it's her turn. The light turns red. The skipping refrain drives her forward.

She notices the homeless. Their dreamy presence. Sleeping quietly in building entrances. She is not alone.

Unexpectantly the load lessens. She feels at home in these late-night streets. At home with what has been offered. *Giant Steps* becomes her game, as she stretches to leap across the murky puddle and reach the curb.

∞

A blue bulb lights the hall. A loose doorknob turns. Home.

A hint of steamy deep-fried from the Chinese restaurant below, the only early morning intruder.

She unfolds the blanket. Takes her pillow from the closet. The couch, her oasis. The living room, her chosen turf.

She finds the turntable on. The needle circling the

record label in homage. Jaco spins.

The rhythms of John – Jocko – Jaco wander into her dreams.

∞

The ultimate bassist, born in Pennsylvania. Though his name and appearance reflected his otherworldliness. Jaco. Jaco Pastorius.

Early photos reveal a young boy. Through the dappled light of a summer backyard. Just another suburban kid. In love with music and Tracey.

He embraces the *Bass of Doom*. His first and only bass. His only bass until thirty years later when it was stolen. Unattended. As he observed a neighborhood basketball game. Distracted by the street.

He called frets speed bumps. They just got in the way. Slowed him down. They say he removed the frets of his bass with a kitchen knife. Shed the confines of everything that had been known before him. Playing dangerous stuff everyone else was afraid to try. His vision, unbounded.

A rebellious genius with an extraordinary cause. He played so hard he changed his strings with each performance. The beat. It drove him hard. His fervor, a fever.

∞

Waking at noon to movements in the kitchen. Traffic in the streets below. She wonders. Without speed bumps, what would happen when you encounter a rock in your path. How do you maneuver the heights? Navigate the depths? When you approach the proverbial rock, do you roll?

She reminds herself of what she has heard. Time after time. That practicing slowly reigns. Above all when the final tempo appears a joke, un scherzo. The far end of the spectrum.

∞

Jaco's bass solo, *Portrait of Tracy*, rendered everything lighter, softer.

Uncanny harmonics. Strung together with a fine thread of devotion. His elusiveness questioning limitations of perception.

Chords surfacing. Dissolving. A touch of the familiar in his unique genius. An intimacy. Just Jaco and his bass. As if there were no other.

∞

She deciphers the illusion created by his harmonics.

Just map out where they're found on the fretboard. Then translate them notewise. Once you've located and decoded the harmonics, it's simple to mix them into the melody. Fill out the harmony. There are only so many of them. Planets in a similar solar system. Offering an alternative dimension.

A pacifying ease descends. She feels close to the source. Jaco's revolution, both her captivation and freedom.

∞

Lessons learned:

Practice your scales.

Take it slow.

And watch
your

step.

∞

She stands on a bridge separating boroughs. The deep roar of cars rumbles beneath her feet. A vague hope spirals up her body.

She witnesses the water streaming toward her. The East River flowing south. The fragile present transforming into the rumination of a vague future.

Past the Statue of Liberty. To the ocean.

Out beyond her sight.

∞

The records continue to spin. Needle spiraling toward the center. Nowhere but home.

Back to the beginning. Thunder and lightning. The birth of the bass electric.

Back to BB and the black vinyl couch. The simplicity of his solo guitar, her first love. He makes Lucille sing, as if there were no deeper infatuation. If love is nothing but his blues, how blue can she get?

Her bass. Beet red. Heavy in her hands.

The Bassoon

The Hills

Whether
the bassoon was
unearthed
or
invented
is a matter of
perspective.

Genuine
in its imperfect intonation
its timbre
a gentle infusion
porous
as mist.

A transcendence of intention
uninhibited
by human interference.

Or so
it sounds.

∽

She opens a hard case. Lined in maroon velvet. A musty whisper, reminiscent of prayer greets her. The resonant intimacy of wooden pews and padded kneelers, darkened from wear. Something sacred. Tenuous.

She takes each long wooden tube and fits them together. Lining up the lowest B flat key with the ivory rimmed bell. Locking the wing joint. Wiggling in the corked bocal. Retrieving the soaked reed.

Breathing deeply. Hands well-positioned. She starts from stillness.

∽

Her first bassoon is a public-school instrument. Resin rather than wood. To maintain that she resents the fact that they advise her not to play the bassoon, observing her size and age, is an understatement. She embraces its muted dense tone, disregarding the predetermined attitudes of others.

That is not to say she doesn't struggle.

The left thumb alone is responsible for eight keys. She makes peace with the enormity of the task. Sliding down to the lowest notes, managing the whisper key and lock, then cautiously climbing the higher register.

She carries the heavy case on her walk to and from school. Commuting for her lessons, through crowded subways, up and down never-ending flights of stairs. Switching hands every block. Her palms calloused. Weathering her tenacity, no matter the severity of the storm.

As years pass, her respect for the bassoon magnifies. A trusted anchor in a life that tends to unravel at the edges. The bassoon's complexity, her simplicity.

∞

Some say the first bassoon surfaced in the 16th century. A single piece of wood, not four.

In the early 17th century, the young woodwind appeared in a wide range of forms, from 15 inches to 4 feet 9 inches. It was the French who later transformed it into a four-piece instrument, resembling the present-day bassoon.

∽

The midday sun beats hard
On my back.
A small café offers
Both shade and today's newspaper.

∽

The world turns. Her feet savor the cool water of a foreign garden spring. She gazes up through the summer heat through the silver-green haze of olive trees. Toward the still line of cypress.

Fig trees dot the hillside. Fruit filling the branches. A telltale drop of syrup held in suspension, testament to ripeness.

She slips up the hill though the basil of her garden. Past tomatoes, then garlic. Opens the door onto cool ceramic tiles stained red with wax. Dante greets her, tail wagging. Wet nose in the palm of her hand.

She lifts her bassoon from the table. Arranges the sheets on the music stand. Vivaldi. Concerto in F Major lifts through the roof tiles, accompanied by the coo of doves.

Her shepherd howls.

∞

She washes the dishes in the stone sink listening to Puccini.

An early memory surfaces. Her grandfather winds his gramophone, after polishing the wooden horn. He places the record gently on the turnstile. Caruso. Only Caruso. Only on Sundays.

He sits, head back. Then swivels in the wooden chair at his desk. Taken back to his origins. The Italy of his youngest years. Perhaps even earlier. To the Italy of his parents. Before things changed. For them.

He watches her tenderly. No words. The air saturated by this rare moment of rapture. An unexpected state of grace for a man drained by disenchantments.

∞

I sit at one
Of the two
Round tables
And watch a woman slowly wash white dishes.
Blurred by the flowing
Open faucet
Her pale hands
Becoming the moon of the plates.
I finish my coffee
And continue
My day's journey.

∞

Italy. What was once the nightmare of past generations, a delirium that sparked mass migrations, has become her reality, her sanity. An unexpected translucence after a series of initiations by fire that scarred her life.

What doesn't kill you can push you toward the edge of the flat existence as we know it, push us toward the soft underbelly of an accommodating charmed beast, that sooths our soulful search.

Pushing known elements to the periphery and leaving purely the present. A reverie rooted in reality. One we can touch. Our own hard-won discovery. The Old World.

∞

Bassoon in Italian is *fagotto*. Literally translated: a bundle. A handful.

So true to term. Various pieces held together with the help of corked fittings and locks. Hidden amidst an army of keys.

∞

As she carries in logs for the fire, she imagines their genetic connection with her *fagotto*. A bundle filling her arms. To be thrown into the stove. Setting off a liberation of sparks. The alchemy of cooking over fire. The resulting golden comfort.

Her music is no different. Breath rising out of the cherry stained wood. The allure of a trill and resolution. The intuition of a well-placed grace note.

∽

The windows mist over as the room heats. She struggles to unearth her inspiration, quiet in the dormant Tuscan countryside.

New York City. So far away. There, the energy swept her up. With or without permission. She just needed to steer clear. Orchestrate her movements. But the pulse wasn't her own. She simply tuned into the river of energy, the city's unrelenting heart-beat. Trying hard to keep her head above water.

To manage the thrill of competition while avoiding its destructive potential.

∽

In these hills, she encounters other challenges. She struggles to occupy the hours of the day, like buckets needing to be filled. So much space. At times. Deafening.

She searches churches. Their cool stone floor and ribs of pews. Black and white marble patterns. A well-defined belly of a beast. Offering needed perspective.

She spends her days in the company of Pontormo. His strong and centered women. Solid as the columns of a cathedral. His *Visitation* sustains her. Embraces her as she acquires depth within their phenomenal dimensions and saturated tones.

∞

The Renaissance search to place an individual within a flexible system of animate and inanimate objects. Recognizing our ability to ascend and descend a hierarchy at will. A rebellious act. Threatening the powers that be.

As does the depiction of veils. So transparent yet protective. Or the clear water painted delicately over bare feet. There and not there. Just a shimmer.

Giving permission to consciously forget one's past and join something more universally collective. Not the rhythm of the city but the ebbs and flow of history.

∞

The night
Climbed in my

Window
And found me
As a firefly flew
Around my head.
I slept
Until again
The night left me
Full.

∞

A succession of full moons pass. Years of white dishes washed in the mist of landscape. Stored within the structure of cultivated land.

The past begins to blur behind her. She becomes restless. The orange light of the afternoon no longer fills her present to the edge.

Winding through the hills. Concentrating around blind curves. The *ginestra* blooming along the roadside as a guardrail. Its scent mind-altering.

She enters the fields. Walks toward the tortured trunks of olive trees. Feeling their muted sorrow.

She waits till the new moon rises. The darkness, a screen allowing her quandary to materialize. Does paradise become a prison once the fear of leaving closes doors, shuts windows?

Once you realize you have forgotten the pathway home, is the visitation over?

∞

Her family's voyage scarred generations. Weaving a distressed map over their chests. A primal tear cut deep.

Trauma reappearing throughout decades, sinister as a serpent circling to bite its own tale, just when it feels a mitigating hint of evolution. Swallowing a family whole, were it not for the relentless acts of kindness based in love which define our nature.

Riding a wave of hope across the Atlantic. Leaving their entire world behind for the shadow of a dream. Without knowing who promised the land. Or whose land it was.

∞

She sits at the kitchen table. Her Olivetti in front of

her. A typewriter bought in Ferrara, gently defined by the Po River.

Ferrara. Where Ariosto once lived. Author of the *Orlando Furioso.* A Renaissance poet who questioned the epic vision, clearing the trail for Cervantes to write the first modern novel.

He chronicled the journey of Astolfo. Flying high on the mythical hippogryph. Front half eagle. Hind half horse. Flying to the moon where all lost things are preserved. Lost objects, lost promises, lost memories, lost minds.

Astolfo searched for the wits of Orlando and found them well labeled in a small flask. Returned the hero's ability to reason.

The deed was done. And literary history rolled on, leaving the epic verse to rest.

∞

It is not her wits she wishes to retrieve but her memories. To quiet the chorus in her head. The chorus of centuries. Always present amidst these hills so weighted by the past. She doesn't plan to fly to the moon but call words to the surface.

To define the importance of her personal history may seem inconsequential when constantly faced with the monumental relics of previous periods. The astonishing creations of great minds.

She needs to add to tradition with a fresh sword in stone, a marker dug deep into her present. To claim her place on the timeline, no matter how complex and trivial her involvement. And so, she writes...

The Forgetful Man

Trees stir memories; live waters heal them.
Annie Dillard

There once was a man with a very bad memory.

One day, he went to the doctor and said, "Doctor, by now I've lived many years yet never seem to learn from my mistakes. I run into the same problems without re-membering past remedies. I have grown tired."

The doctor told him to buy a simple notebook and return

the next week.

The next week, the forgetful man returned with his new notebook and asked the doctor what to do next. The doctor replied that he should begin to write down his everyday experiences in detail and return the next week. The forgetful man agreed and the session ended.

What he didn't tell the doctor was that he didn't know how to write, or, to be truthful, he had forgotten. Embarrassed by this fact, he never returned yet he always carried his notebook with him, just hoping.

It all started in late spring when the forgetful man found himself in the midst of a strangely beautiful moment. The flowers were blooming. Donkeys were grazing in the tall swaying grass. A banjo's melody rambled from the neighboring hills. He couldn't tell where his fingers ended and the afternoon began.

Desperately, he took out his notebook and ripped out a blank page. He held it high above his head, in the sky, overlooking the valley, and then quickly folded it, until small enough to fit in his pocket. When he returned home, he placed the folded sheet in a shoe box beneath his bed. He felt safer as he slept that night.

A few days later, his best friend telephoned him. He had forgotten her birthday and was the only one absent from the party. The candles drooped anxiously as did the guests. Right away, the forgetful man sent his best friend a bouquet of roses. "How many times have these flowers been sent and I continue to forget!" he cried helplessly, covering his face with his hands.

Without thinking, he ripped out another page from his notebook and carefully exposed it to the dark, closed air of his room, folded it up, first in halves, then quarters, then eighths, placed it in the shoe box, turned off the light and fell asleep. In the morning, his head ached slightly yet he had forgotten the box beneath the bed.

The forgetful man continued to gather both happy and sad moments of his life. He stored them without ever noticing that he has become a collector of sorts.

Finally, one day, when he needed it most, he realized. It was a short day in mid-February. The sun had already begun to set, when the forgetful man found himself in a part of the city before then, unknown to him. He tried to follow the street signs but they all appeared written in some foreign tongue with indecipherable letters that only took him in circles, deeper and deeper into confusion. He searched for hours on end. The streets slithered like snakes under the light rain. He had forgotten his umbrella.

Somehow, magically he arrived home. As he opened the door to his apartment, everything whirled in newness. He saw things as if never seen before: the delicate flower print of his faded curtain, the golden design of the picture frame, the curve of the faucet as it held the last drop of water in breathless suspension and the grey cardboard box beneath his small unmade bed.

He pulled out the dusty box. He found it filled with folded sheets of paper. And then, he remembered.

He unfolded the yellow pages and hung each one up on the clothesline which cut his room in two. Slowly, surely, images began to appear: a donkey braying in the wind, a bouquet of yellow roses, a plaid umbrella, yet as slowly as each memory revealed itself, it slowly fled, running down the paper and dripping in vivid colors onto the floor.

Once again, the pages hung blankly, but a glistening lake remained, in the middle of the room. Every morning, the man took pleasure in wading through its waters and often stood calmly at its center.

∾

The bassoon's soft call beckons from both shores. The *Sarabande* of Bach's Cello Suite number V. Lines descending, trickling, with a final lifting suspension. A welcome accompaniment that tempers her return.

She accepts the nonlinear quality of her life. The zigzag of a journey. Collecting the breadcrumbs before they sink.

She pictures herself walking though crystalline water, her feet visible as she steps over smooth stones, until she reaches her painstakingly circumscribed understanding of home.

Within these waters, she encounters a baptism of clarity. Light as a dove's feather. She breaths deeply as if to inhale the phenomenon. Ingest the deep sense of congruence.

Caruso Sundays surface. Her grandmother's soft accent. Her mother's roasted peppers. The undeniably complex sense of home reflected in their dark tired eyes. Their melancholic ways and strong small hands.

∞

In early music, the bassoon was scored as an essential foundation. No need for a metronome or compass. A place to rest. To rest assured.

Humble and generous in its underappreciated compulsion, the bassoon allowed a harmonizing layering over reliable roots. A solid substitution for the bass pedals of the organ. An organ outlawed in English cathedrals in the 1600s, as an instrument of superstition and idolatry.

Little did they know.

Little did we know the future of the bassoon. The transcendence of Donizetti's furtive *lagrima*. Or the tendency toward transgression captured in the solo opening of *The Rite of Spring*.

Tenuous
as an echo

Dangerously distant
as a memory

Threatening to materialize. From the deepest rings of our existence.

The Harp

The Woods

From the tombs of Egyptian pharaohs and temples of Babylon. The harp appeared. An adaptation of the bow, a relic of the hunt. Strings of hair and plant fiber, strung to a hollowed sound box.

A bed of strings. Casting a shadow, precarious as hair across a pillow.

Or cast on ancient stone. A hieroglyph. A missive initiating a story. A tale that travels. That teaches of a place of origin.

Plucked. As the name suggests. The harp.

∞

Her mother plays the harp at her wedding. *Planxty Irwin*. A waltz. Playing with a mother's intention. Bestowing her blessing.

She is the last child to wed. Her mother intuitively trusts the groom. Taking the proverbial leap of faith, as their unexpected romance measures the fragile blink of an eye.

∞

First she tunes the harp. Her hands slightly twisted by age. Lowering the tone, then lifting to pitch. An undeniable settling into place. String by string. Preparing the bed of cords to a delicate perfection before even starting. To play.

Her right-hand fingers reach for the melody. Hooking and releasing. The left, creating a framework of repeating rhythms. A complicated accompaniment for the simplest of compositions.

∞

Learning the harp has the advantage of always sounding celestial. No matter the accuracy. As if a wind chime, the ambiguity, the randomness of the exercise and errors, mirroring nature and its elements. Refreshing in its inimitability. Unrepeatable in its innocence.

Every now and then, a passing child candidly causes the strings to sing.

∞

Before she had children, her own mother was an enigma. Ridden with riddles and rules. Protecting others, risking sense of self.

Now she is a mother, her mother stands exposed in all her fortitude. Resilience before unnoticed. Yet not without a few secrets still up her sleeve. Secrets lace her intricate lullabies, as grandchildren sleep on the carpet by her feet.

∞

Sitting on my mother's back,
in my mother's bed,
gently brushing
my mother's soft short hair.

Small fingers lifting
a few strands
with a colored clip
then letting them fall.
Just the hint of a black wave
against pale cheek.

Feeling my mother's warmth
on inner thighs
through cotton pajamas.
Safe
connected
amidst the waves of pink sheets
and patterned quilt.

A cloudless sky overhead.
As we float
in a timeless space
unchronicled.

∞

She never imagined that her own children would bring her home. That they would build the nest with their breath, their voice. They are the columns of her temple. The chaotic calm at the end of the storm. Rendering the world vibrant. No matter the responsibility.

She leans back in her chair at the shared dinner table. Her mind elusively blending her memories with her children's present lightness. Careful as a surgeon. Without risk of loss.

The window open. Lace curtains float. Music weaving through their laughter. Collected flowers filling vases. Candles burning precariously amidst spilling wax. Forming the wings of angels. Translucent witnesses. Imagined guardians of the moment.

∞

Who would ever imagine
such a simple moment
would form the essence of mother.
Would provide a needed point of reference
when lineage
proves a mere illusion
or delusion.
A point of reference
mollifying
a childhood
of trepidations
and lingering
ambiguity.

∞

Traditionally, harpists traveled through Ireland as

itinerant storytellers. Sharing news and narrative throughout the countryside. Composing melodies and unraveling tales for room and board. Performing for their supper.

The art of storytelling wove the alienated villages into a continuous culture, protecting the oral keepsakes of those hillside communities.

∞

She has read to her children every evening for more than a decade. It seems every book they read together, though chosen randomly, is what they need to read. To hear.

They search for the clue. The coincidence. Most often, it takes them by surprise. Hidden within a dense paragraph or description. Just when they imagine this specific story might be the exception to the rule.

The books come to a close. All is quiet. They listen to the resonance of those last words. Savor the world they had the opportunity to appropriate, even if simply for the span of a finite number of chapters. Before falling asleep.

∞

At night her mother maintains the silence of the tempered light. She abandons her harp and retires to her loom. Without risking waking her grandchildren, her hands work horizontally across the vertical framework, wool pulled taut. Weaving the mixed memories of the day. Twigs and dried weeds from the woods. Twisted promises and whispered truths. Bath oils and evening tea.

She combines the obscure with the effervescent. The forgiving with the intolerant. Until a variegated repetition surfaces. She recognizes it as sincere. And sets it with warm tears.

As the night slides toward increased stillness, she cannot help but intertwine her forebodings concerning the future. Apprehension of the unknown. Trepidation regarding her own mortality. When the last petal falls and her hands lay silent, how will they manage without her? The resulting pattern threatens the evolution of her design, endangering their collective narrative.

The daughter wakes before dawn. Leaving her children asleep, their breath heavy, warm against silent pillows. Eyes barely open, she quietly reaches for the loom. Feels the blended recollections of the initial composition, the coarse texture of the final rows.

In what has become her morning mission, she carefully unravels her mother's foreboding finale. Unweaving what was woven out of fear of an uncertain future. Gathering the dismantled prophecies in a basket by her feet.

Their shared tapestry remains. Document to the past and present. Protected from midnight worries that dissolve in the first morning light. Worries buried deep in the backyard. Behind the rosebushes. Carefully forgotten. Left unsung.

∞

The harp. The loom. A solicitation. Invoking a veneration of folklore. A breadth of widespread strings, chords. Brought to life. With divergent movements.

The harp and the loom. The medium for the message. A code to decipher. Exposing a pattern, hiding a warning. Inciting rebellion. Or simply announcing a birth, or death. Journeying miles to reach its designated recipient.

The harpist, a rebel. Synchronizing the blue, red and clear strings. Modeling a memorandum. Syncopating smoke signals. A call to action.

The weaver. Bearing the same burden. Setting to stone. The missive, an irrefutable artifact.

∞

As Santa Lucia helps those unable to see what is staring them in the face, the daughter ultimately unwraps the blinders from her eyes. Searching for the courage to read the writing on the wall.

The alarming conclusions on the loom continue. The daughter is no longer able to routinely unweave them. Without taking notice of her mother's weakening steps and loss of breath, weight.

The prophesies turn to reality as her mother drifts to the sea of an irreversible destiny. The daughter forced to watch. No remedy at hand. No miracle. This challenge without a solution.

The mother is frightened into silence. Never acknowledging in words, her near future. She no longer plays the harp for her grandchildren but sings songs from her childhood to those she imagines as her audience. The children listen patiently, incongruity unnoticed.

The daughter searches for a new mythology. A digestible fable to explain the inevitable to her two children. When the fragile moral of the story breaks under the weight of circumstance.

∞

In the early morning, they crawl into their grandmother's bed, listening for her breath. Reaching for the warmth of her body. Blowing on her eyelids. Conjuring her eyes to open.

In a last flash of lucidity, the grandmother reaches in front of her. Opening her eyes wide. Looking for the key. The grandchildren let her go as she finds the door. Opens the latch.

∞

A flutter
is barely audible
as I search
your heartbeat.

As futile
as capturing
rain falling
or night lifting.

There is no telling
where you fly
as I let go
of a dream
held so tight
it can't breathe.

Your powder
On my hands
Silent witness.

∞

Her mother personified perseverance. Learning the harp at a later age. After her daughters had gone.

Already a grandmother.

Trusting evolution and familiar curiosity, she leaves the harp to her daughter. A silent agreement. Never discussed. Understood.

The daughter closes her eyes and listens before playing. Listening for a voice captured. An echo caught in a wooden frame. A small red bird against the windowpane. Whispering a message.

Her mother is left to rest in the relative peace of a melodious recollection. Her daughter inheriting her well-rooted intuition. Her fingers slowly follow. Obeying a resounding tradition. Stretching over hills. Across thresholds.

∞

The journey of the harpist provides nothing less than a needed network. Bearing simple exchanges, developing historically layered storytelling, revealing conspiracies citing rebellion.

Lessons surface and lives are put on the line. The thin line of a melody exposing the need of the people, the needs of one person. A space where the most feared circumstances find a necessary home, a safe haven for communication.

The door cracks open. A note is entrusted. A feather falls. The harmony hides the blade within. Renders it readable. Softening the impact.

The Concertina

The Mountains

Polygonal in form. the concertina fits intimately in the player's palms. Extending then compressing, hands work the central bellows. The heart of the instrument. Sending air over internal reeds.

∞

The small square case arrives in the evening. She never tells her father she's received it. The next morning, he dies.

She takes his concertina from the box. Can still feel the warmth of his promise. Her hands small in comparison. Lost in his space.

Her fingertips slip off polished buttons. It will take time before she is at ease with the positioning. Finds the basic rhythm. The push and pull. Time before she trusts the hidden mechanisms.

She begins with simple ballads her father sang.

Protest songs from the sixties. Flowers gone and sorrowful men. It becomes her alternative voice. Her hammer in the morning. Her bell in the evening.

∾

The German concertina found its way to Ireland as the Great Famine ended. In the humblest Irish households, you could find a concertina. Purring the essence of native melodies. Soothing the wounds of deprivation and separation due to immigration.

∾

There is so much new about her life. Their children have left. Following the flight of the swallows to the north. Their home rings with a deeper tone. More space. And silence.

They are alone. And share nights of blooming jasmine. An affection as grounded as huitlacoche. Both superficial yet profound. They swing in the loosely woven hammock. Strung wall to wall. A chrysalis of tenderness. Announcing the rainy season.

∽

You are

The columns of my temple.
The water in my flow.
The midnight in my darkness.
The angel in the snow.

The wisdom of my madness.
The whisper of my cry.
The thunder of my lightning.
The apple of my eye.

∽

After the desert blooms, the dry season retreats. They pray for the storm clouds to roll over the mountains. In their direction. After so much patient watering.

Eventually, she learns folk songs from his land. Ballads from south of the border. Unearthed from a rebellious tradition. Narratives of hardships and hopes so essential, they cry with the summer's first rains. With the early evening rivers that fill the narrow streets.

She whispers the words in Spanish to help find the pattern of breath. To shape the movement of the bellows. Careful not to twist in exaggeration. To synchronize the short phrasing. As her slight arms close, then open.

∞

In the villages, there was always a fiddle and concertina playing. As bees swarm or birds flock, everyone seemed to play a concertina. As natural as mowing a meadow or dancing a jig in front of the evening fire.

∞

She feels the presence of those she has lost. And those who have purposefully wandered.

Her adult children, nomads with clear missions. Testing foreign ground. Caught between languages.

She dares not ask them the vernacular of their dreams. Not wishing to stir calming waters. Or question which streets are beneath their feet. Their purposeful process deserving of respect.

Their breath is the same. One breath. One love. No matter the dimension or dialect uttered. El mismo canto.

∞

But my love never changes
No matter the distance
Neither the memory, or the pain
Of my country, my people.

∞

The sweet fiddle, buoyant banjo and rambling concertina were often grounded by the soft shuffle of improvised percussion on any available surface.

Bands played in the streets for Sunday crowds. Or accompanied the rails to sooth the needier passengers. Mingling with meager meals and tales of their homeland changing before their very eyes.

∞

There were times she felt as if she were the train. Unidentifiable details of the landscape, a blur of cities and fields, alluded her. The elements of her existence, ajumble. Her life, high-speed.

As her present extends and she witnesses the exits and entrances of those surrounding her, she identifies more with the landscape. A peaceful motionless perspective. The setting of a stage.

Allowing for the game pieces to move.
Being the board.

Offering a semblance of order so essential.
An alphabet.
She is the *casa*, the street, the patio.

The train speeds through. Across her small frame. And she lets go. Stays put. Watching it move toward the horizon. And disappear.

The rumble intensifies in its proximity. Then diminuendos as it departs. Leaving her heart swayed but sustained by the fragile grass beneath her feet.

2

Seconds
like crickets
tick.
Golondrinas sweep.

The rain clears
the dust from the leaves
as they fall like years
and drift behind us.

Una migración
marked by left objects
my mother's rosaries
my father's furia
a family photograph.

Across a patchwork of states
and countries
each their own color
mi cuerpo su mapa
borders and rivers
and random consequences.

Our love deepens
as tea leaves brew
steeping a darkly fragrant force
stirring
the lives of those
we touch.

∞

Settling into the landscape. Watching the weather evolve overhead. The extremes of soft clouds, then dramatic thunderstorms. She remains rooted to her present. Toes dug deep into the sandy desert soil.

The table set. An invitation. Soft music playing. Colored windows and wooden doors open. Transparent curtains drifting in the breeze.

She bakes her cake with nuts and berries. Slivers of chocolate. And lays it on the table. An offering, in the center of her grandmother's stained lace table-cloth. She sits at the table. Facing the door. Napkin on her lap.

∞

What has changed yesterday
May change again tomorrow
As we continue to change
In these faraway lands.

∞

Some days, many guests arrive. Too many to count. Some days, just one.

Some days, her guests just linger. Peering through the windows. From the door. And do not enter.

Some guests relay a message. Others expect one. Some come in silence. A message. Implicit.

Some days, the train goes straight through their home. Without stopping. She waves. The back door left open.

∞

The concertina, humble in size. Diminutive. A little concert. A small pause. Between memory and expectation.

An instant for reflection. Marking the here and now. A milestone. Perhaps just a millimeter, at our disposal.

Where the present begs forgiveness. Begs gratitude. Amidst a sea of uncertainty.

The concertina.

Bric-a-Brac

Press